By Karla Kuskin · Illustrated by Melissa Iwai

Green as a Bean

LAURA GERINGER BOOKS
An Imprint of HarperCollins*Publishers*

Green as a Bean

Text copyright © 1960, 2007 by Karla Kuskin   Illustrations copyright © 2007 by Melissa Iwai
Manufactured in China by South China Printing Company Ltd.   All rights reserved. No part of
this book may be used or reproduced in any manner whatsoever without written permission except
in the case of brief quotations embodied in critical articles and reviews. For information address
HarperCollins Children's Books, a division of HarperCollins Publishers, 1350 Avenue of the
Americas, New York, NY 10019.   www.harpercollinschildrens.com

Library of Congress Cataloging-in-Publication Data
Kuskin, Karla.
    [Square as a house]
    Green as a bean / by Karla Kuskin ; illustrated by Melissa Iwai.— 1st ed.
        p.   cm.
    "The text of this book was originally published in 1960 under the title Square as a house"—T.p.
verso.
    Summary: Questions in verse about the many things you could be if you were square or soft or
loud or red or small or fat or fierce or dark.
    ISBN-10: 0-06-075332-3 (trade bdg.) — ISBN-13: 978-0-06-075332-0 (trade bdg.)
    ISBN-10: 0-06-075334-X (lib. bdg.) — ISBN-13: 978-0-06-075334-4 (lib. bdg.)
    [1. Stories in rhyme.] I. Iwai, Melissa, ill. II. Title.
PZ8.3.K96Sq 2007   2005017881
[E]—dc22   CIP
                                                                                                        AC

Typography by Neil Swaab   3 4 5 6 7 8 9 10   ❖   First Edition
Portions of the text of this book were originally published in 1960
under the title Square as a House.

If you could be green
would you be a lawn
or a lean green bean
and the stalk it's on?

Would you be a leaf
on a leafy tree?
Tell me, lean green one,
what would you be?

If you could be square
would you be a box
containing a cake

or a house
or blocks
with painted letters
from A to Z?

If you could be soft
would you be the snow
or twenty-five pillows

Tell me, fair square one,
what would you be?

or breezes that blow
the blossoms that fall from
the sassafras tree?

Tell me, sweet soft one,
what would you be?

If you could be loud
would you be the sound
of thunder at night

or the howl of a hound
as he bays at the moon
or the pound of the sea?

Tell me, proud loud one,
what would you be?

If you could be small
would you be a mouse
or a mouse's child

or a mouse's house
or a mouse's house's
front door key?

Tell me all, small one,
what would you be?

If you could be red
would you be a car
that races the wind

or jam in a jar
or an acrobat's tights
with a hole in the knee?

Tell me, O red one,
what would you be?

If you could be fierce
and roar with rage
would you be a tiger
and pace your cage?

Would you be a dragon
or two or three?
Tell me, most fierce one,
what would you be?

If you could be blue
would you be the sky
or some early clouds
and three birds up high

or one blue eye
that winks at me?
Tell me, big blue one,
what would you be?

If you could be bright
would you be the sun

Or a starry night
or a thousand and one
fireflies flying
and flickering free?

Tell me, quite bright one,
what would you be?

If you could be somebody
holding a book
who looked just exactly
the way that you look,
who turned all these pages
and then said, "I'm through,"

tell me, my dear one,
would you be you?

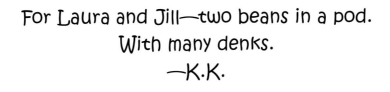

For Laura and Jill—two beans in a pod.
With many denks.
—K.K.

For Jamie, my favorite little green bean.
—M.I.